Webster

written by
Martin Waddell

For Emily, Daniel and Katie—M.W.

For Danny—D.P.

First published 2001 by Walker Books Ltd, 87 Vauxhall Walk, London SE11 5HJ

This edition published 2002   10 9 8 7 6 5

Text © 2001 Martin Waddell   Illustrations © 2001 David Parkins

This book has been typeset in ITC Tiffany   Printed in China   All rights reserved

British Library Cataloguing in Publication Data:
a catalogue record for this book is available from the British Library

ISBN 978-0-7445-8924-5

www.walker.co.uk

J. Duck

illustrated by
David Parkins

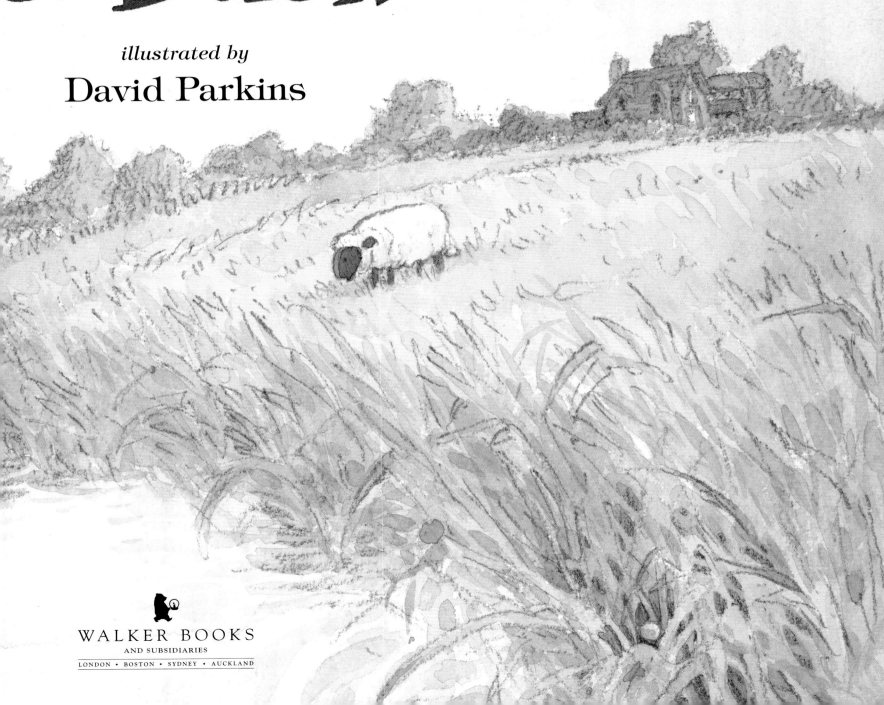

WALKER BOOKS
AND SUBSIDIARIES
LONDON · BOSTON · SYDNEY · AUCKLAND

There was once

a duck egg hidden away in the
reeds by the bank of the lake.
In the duck egg was wee
Webster J. Duck all folded up
so he'd fit in the egg.

Webster stirred
in the egg.

He tapped the eggshell
with his beak and ...

C-R-A-C-K!
The shell broke.

Out of the egg came
wee Webster J. Duck.

Webster J. Duck stood on the
bits of shell he had broken.
"Where is my mum?" Webster thought.
"I must have a mum,
because all baby ducks do."

Webster went

"Quack-
quack,
quack-
quack!"

calling his mum,

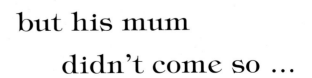

but his mum
didn't come so ...

MARTIN WADDELL says of *Webster J. Duck*, "It's a sunny story born of
long holidays with my children by a lake on the River Shannon in Ireland.
We saw a nest in the reeds, a watchful cow in the mud by the lakeside,
and a small duck. In that moment, Webster's story was born."

Martin Waddell has written many books for children, including the picture
books *Farmer Duck* and *Can't You Sleep, Little Bear?*, both of which won the Smarties Book Prize.
He has also won the Best Books for Babies Award, the Kurt Maschler Award and the Hans Christian
Andersen Award. His other titles include *Who Do You Love?*, *The Hollyhock Wall*, *Owl Babies*,
A Kitten Called Moonlight, *Tom Rabbit* and many stories for older readers.
Martin Waddell lives in Northern Ireland.

DAVID PARKINS has illustrated numerous children's books, including six
stories by Dick King-Smith about a little girl called Sophie and the picture
books *No Problem*, *Aunt Nancy and Old Man Trouble*, *Aunt Nancy and
Cousin Lazybones*, *Prowlpuss* (shortlisted for the 1994 Kurt Maschler Award
and the 1995 Smarties Book Prize) and *Fly Traps! Plants that Bite Back*
(shortlisted for the TES Junior Information Book Award).
He is married with three children and lives in Canada.

Webster J. Duck set off to find her.

Webster met a Duck with a Waggledy Tail,
down by the side of the lake.

"Quack-quack?"
asked Webster J. Duck.

"Bow-wow!"

went the Duck with the Waggledy Tail.

"You're not my mum," Webster thought.
"My mum would go quack-quack
like me!"

Next Webster met a Big Woolly Duck.

"Quack-quack?"
asked Webster J. Duck.

"Baa-baa!"
went the Big Woolly Duck.

"You're not my mum," Webster
thought. "My mum would go
quack-quack like me!"

Then Webster met a Bigger Big Duck,
with big ears and an udder.

"Quack-quack?"
asked Webster J. Duck.

"Moo-moo!"
went the Bigger Big Duck.

"You're not my mum," Webster
thought. "My mum would go
quack-quack like me!"

Webster J. Duck sat down and cried
by the edge of the lake.
His little duck feathers were shiny
with tiny duck tears.

"Quack, quack, quack,"
sobbed Webster.

"BOW-WOW!"

barked the Duck with
the Waggledy Tail.

"BAA-BAA!"

baa-ed the Big
Woolly Duck.

"MOO-MOO-MOO-MOO!"

moo-ed the Bigger Big Duck.

They were trying to help by

calling his mum ...

but the BOW-WOWs and
the BAAs and the MOOs
scared Webster J. Duck.
He hid his little duck
head under his wing,
and he quivered
and shivered and
shook and he went
"Quack-quack,"
all alone.

And then someone answered
"QUACK-QUACK!"
(just like Webster's quack, but
quite a bit louder).

QUACK-QUACK! QUACK

Mum Duck came through
the reeds.

And Webster swam off
with his mum.